HUSH UP

and migrate!

Design by Shan Stumpf

ISBN: 978-1-943978-42-7

10 9 8 7 6 5 4 3 2 1

Printed in the United States of America

cpsia tracking label information
Production Location: CG Book Printers
North Mankato, Minnesota
Production Date: February 2020
Cohort: Batch № 294310

Produced by Persnickety Press
An imprint of WunderMill, inc.
120A North Salem Street
Apex, NC 27502

*The author would like to thank the
following people for sharing their
enthusiasm and expertise: Dr. Kerry
Nicholson and Dr. Lincoln Parrett,
Alaska Department of Fish and Game,
Wildlife Conservation Division. A special
thank-you to Skip Jeffery for his loving
support during the creative process.*

WunderMillBooks.com

HUSH
UP
and migrate!

by Sandra Markle

illustrated by Howard McWilliam

PERSNICKETY
PRESS

Mama Caribou looks down
at the tiny green sprout
peeking out of the snowdrift.
"I see spring coming, Baby Bou,"
she tells her calf.
"It's time to migrate."

"But, Mama," Baby Bou says.
"My friends are waiting. I have to play."

"Arrrrr!" Mama Caribou grunts then says, "I guess we can stay a *little* longer before we head north for the summer."

She watches Baby Bou run and romp and race
with the other calves until a flock of swans flies past.

Then Mama Caribou lifts her head, and her
big ears turn as she listens to their whistles.

"I hear spring coming," she calls to her calf.
"It's time to migrate."

"But, Mama, I'm hungry."

Mama Caribou says, "I guess we can eat before we start north."
Then she sniffs until she finds lichens under the snow,
and, shoveling with her hooves, uncovers their meal.

Side-by-side, the pair munches the snow-crusted lichens while the bright sun warms their backs.

"I feel spring coming,"
Mama Caribou says.
"It's time to migrate.
And that's a good thing.

Remember all the tasty food on our summer range:

grass,

willow leaves,

flowers,

and your favorite—
mushrooms."

Baby Bou wrinkles his nose.
"I remember there were also lots of..."

"MOSQUITOES!"

Baby Bou bawls, "I'm not going! Migrating is *boring!* All we do is walk. Walk. Walk. Walk. WALK! I'm staying here with my friends for the summer."

Mama Caribou says,
"Bou, dear, your friends
will be migrating too.
And, without the herd,
how will you stay safe from
prowling bears and hunting wolves?"

"I can take care of myself."
Baby Bou lifts his head
to show off the spikes that
are his growing antlers.

"Besides, I'm a fast runner.
A strong swimmer.
And I'm super at hiding.
You go ahead, Mama.
Migrate without me."

"Okay, but you'll miss your big surprise,"
Mama Caribou calls as she trots off.

"A surprise?"
Baby Bou gallops to catch up.
"What surprise?!"

Mama Caribou says, "I'm expecting a calf. So, when we reach our summer range, you'll be Big Bou to a new baby brother or sister."

"Whoopee!"

"Well, then, hush up and *migrate.*"

Baby Bou trots alongside his mother.
And, grunting so they can keep track of each other, they join
the herd to head north toward the caribou's summer range.

"Mama!" Baby Bou calls from where he's standing with all four hooves firmly planted.

"What is it, dear?"

WHY DO CARIBOU MIGRATE?

Each year, many caribou migrate (travel long distances between two home ranges). In the spring, they trek to the Arctic tundra, a large, nearly treeless area. They go there because the cool temperatures and continual sunlight that cause the green plants to grow slowly. Because of the slow growth, the plants are more nutritious than the faster growing plants farther south. Caribou mothers need the energy boost that food supplies to produce the protein-rich milk their calves need to grow up.

In the far north, there are also fewer predators (hungry hunters), such as grizzly bears, wolves, and golden eagles to catch and kill their calves. Plus, there's safety in being part of a big herd. One calf among thousands has a much greater chance of escaping predators.

Caribou could stay on the tundra year-round, and some do. Their double fur coat, which even covers their noses, lets them stand the extreme cold. But for those that do migrate south to a winter range, the deep snow that piles up is softer. It's easier for them to dig down to the ground and the lichens they mainly eat during the winter. Plus, by staying on the move, the herd of hungry caribou continues to find food rather than eating up every bit of food in just one area.

There are four main caribou herds that migrate each spring and fall. One of the largest and farthest trekking is the Porcupine caribou herd, named for the Porcupine River they cross while migrating. This herd numbers about 169,000 animals, and travels about 400 miles between its winter and summer ranges. In fact, the Porcupine caribou herd holds the record for the longest overland migration.

Beaufort Sea

Prudhoe Bay

Kaktovik

Nuiqsut

SUMMER LOCATION

SPRING MIGRATION

FALL MIGRATION

DETAIL ALASKA

Arctic Village

WINTER LOCATION

ALASKA

Coldfoot

WHERE ARE THE OTHER MIGRATORS?

Other animals migrate to the Arctic tundra to raise their young. Many are birds that come for the same reason the caribou do—to find lots of food and a safe place to raise babies. Check this map to spot a few of these migrators.

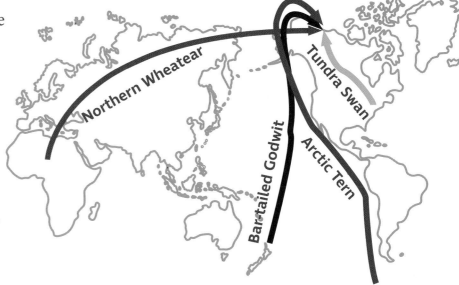

Bar-tailed Godwit
It winters in New Zealand (having flown about 7,200 miles non-stop to get there). In the spring, it stops on the way north and rests in Japan for about a month. The pair's tundra nest is a shallow, grass-lined hollow scraped out of the ground. The female usually lays four eggs that hatch in 20 to 21 days. The parents guard the chicks, but the young are on their own to find food. Like their parents, they eat insects, worms, seeds, and berries.

Tundra Swan
It mainly winters along warmer southern coasts of the United States. A pair mates for life. Back on the tundra, the pair builds a stick nest near water so they can easily feed on the water plants. The female usually lays four eggs that hatch in about 32 days. Both parents lead the chicks to water, paddle, and bring up plants from the bottom for them to eat. The young stay with their parents at least through their first winter.

Northern Wheatear
It winters in Africa. The pair's tundra nest is on the ground, and it's usually a grass-lined hollow under shelter, such as a large rock. The female usually lays five to six eggs that hatch in as little as 14 days. The chicks stay in the nest and are fed by their parents for about 15 more days. Northern Wheatears mainly eat insects.

Arctic Tern
It winters in Antarctica during the continent's summer. The Arctic Tern nests on the ground, with the female laying one to three eggs that hatch in 20 to 21 days. After three days, the chicks leave and hide nearby. Both parents bring them food for about 28 days. The chicks remain with the adults for about two more months.

MIGRATE LIKE A CARIBOU

Just follow these steps to pretend you're a caribou making your spring migration. To really migrate like a caribou, invite your family and friends to trek with you. Then pretend you're a herd and walk the trail single file.

1 **Choose a starting point and an ending point for the migration.** Add four to six chairs, pillows, or other items to make pretend hills and trees. Scatter these between the start and end points.

2 **Use sheets of white paper** to mark a path from the start to the end, making it wind around the hills and trees.

3 **Use blue cloth or blue paper** to add a river to cross along the migration path. Use arm motions to swim as you cross the river.

4 **Mark four or five of the white sheets of paper with an "X".** At those points, a caribou may step off the migration path to rest. Rest only as long as it takes to count out loud from one to five. Others may also stop to rest or pass by until the resting caribou is done counting. As soon as a caribou finishes counting, its rest stop is over, and it must be allowed back on the path. Each migrating caribou must rest at least twice.

5 **Along the trail,** place some self-sealing bags with raisins or other snack food. At any time, a hungry caribou may step off the path to eat. (Only eat one or two bits of the snack food.) After eating and replacing the bag on the trail, the caribou must be allowed back on the path. Each migrating caribou must stop to eat at least twice.

Of course, if you really want to migrate like a caribou, walk the path again—and again—day and night for two weeks. During their spring migration, the caribou herd averages about ten miles a day and keeps on trekking for about 14 days.

EXPLORE MORE! Check out these books and websites to discover even more.

Caribou
www.kidzone.ws/animals/caribou/facts.htm
Facts, photos, and fun activities to download.

Caribou On The Move
www.youtube.com/watch?v=1wB-FhUp0gI
Watch caribou feeding during the snowy winter and then starting to migrate.

Gagne, Tammy. *Caribou* (Animals of North America)
(Mendota Heights, Minnesota: Focus Readers, 2017.)
Find out more about how caribou live in their winter and summer ranges.

Miller, Debbie S. *A Caribou Journey*
(Fairbanks, Alaska: University of Alaska Press, 2010.)
Paintings and text bring the drama of the caribou travel and life through the seasons.

Spring Caribou Migration
www.youtube.com/watch?v=ni8KrZn2LLA
Thousands of caribou migrate north together in the spring.